I0654722

William Wordsworth

A Selection from the Sonnets of William Wordsworth

With Numerous Illustration by Alfred Parsons

William Wordsworth

A Selection from the Sonnets of William Wordsworth
With Numerous Illustration by Alfred Parsons

ISBN/EAN: 9783337275310

Printed in Europe, USA, Canada, Australia, Japan

Cover: Foto ©Andreas Hilbeck / pixelio.de

More available books at **www.hansebooks.com**

A SELECTION from the SONNETS of WILLIAM WORDSWORTH

with numerous ILLUSTRATIONS by ALFRED PARSONS

NEW YORK · HARPER & BROTHERS · PRINTERS &
PUBLISHERS · FRANKLIN SQUARE · M DCCC XCI

Copyright, 1890, by HARPER & BROTHERS.

All rights reserved.

CONTENTS

A SELECTION OF WORDSWORTH'S SONNETS.

FIRST LINES OF SONNETS.

NUNS fret not at their convent's narrow room;
And hermits are contented with their cells;
And students with their pensive citadels;
Maids at the wheel, the weaver at his loom,
Sit blithe and happy; bees that soar for bloom,
High as the highest Peak of Furness-fells,
Will murmur by the hour in foxglove bells:
In truth the prison, unto which we doom
Ourselves, no prison is: and hence for me,
In sundry moods, 'twas pastime to be bound
Within the Sonnet's scanty plot of ground;
Pleased if some Souls (for such there needs must be)
Who have felt the weight of too much liberty,
Should find brief solace there, as I have found.

SCORN not the Sonnet; Critic, you have frowned,
Mindless of its just honours; with this key
Shakspeare unlocked his heart; the melody
Of this small lute gave ease to Petrarch's wound;
A thousand times this pipe, did Tasso sound;
With it Camöens soothed an exile's grief;
The Sonnet glittered a gay myrtle leaf
Amid the cypress with which Dante crowned
His visionary brow: a glow-worm lamp,
It cheered mild Spenser, called from Faeryland
To struggle through dark ways; and, when a damp
Fell round the path of Milton, in his hand
The Thing became a trumpet; whence he blew
Soul-animating strains—alas, too few!

CALM is all nature as a resting wheel.
The kine are couched upon the dewy grass;
The horse alone, seen dimly as I pass,
Is cropping audibly his later meal:
Dark is the ground; a slumber seems to steal
O'er vale and mountain and the starless sky.
Now, in this blank of things, a harmony,
Home-felt, and home-created, comes to heal
The grief for which the senses still supply
Fresh food; for only then, when memory
Is hushed, am I at rest. My friends! restrain
Those busy cares that would allay my pain;
Oh! leave me to myself, nor let me feel
The officious touch that makes me droop again.

I WATCH, and long have watched, with calm regret
Yon slowly-sinking star—immortal Sire—
(So might he seem) of all the glittering quire!
Blue ether still surrounds him—yet—and yet;
But now the horizon's rocky parapet
Is reached, where, forfeiting his bright attire,
He burns—transmuted to a dusky fire—
Then pays submissively the appointed debt
To the flying moments, and is seen no more.
Angels and gods! We struggle with our fate,
While health, power, glory, from their height decline,
Depressed; and then extinguished; and our state,
In this, how different, lost Star, from thine,
That no to-morrow shall our beams restore!

HOW clear, how keen, how marvellously bright
The effluence from yon distant mountain's head,
Which, strewn with snow smooth as the sky can shed,
Shines like another sun—on mortal sight
Uprisen, as if to check approaching Night,
And all her twinkling stars. Who now would tread,
If so he might, yon mountain's glittering head—
Terrestrial, but a surface, by the flight
Of sad mortality's earth-sullying wing,
Unswept, unstained? Nor shall the aerial Powers
Dissolve that beauty, destined to endure,
White, radiant, spotless, exquisitely pure,
Through all vicissitudes, till genial Spring
Has filled the laughing vales with welcome flowers

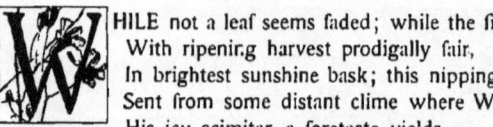

HILE not a leaf seems faded; while the fields,
With ripening harvest prodigally fair,
In brightest sunshine bask; this nipping air,
Sent from some distant clime where Winter wields
His icy scimitar, a foretaste yields
Of bitter change, and bids the flowers beware;
And whispers to the silent birds, "Prepare
Against the threatening foe your trustiest shields."
For me, who under kindlier laws belong
To Nature's tuneful choir, this rustling dry
Through leaves yet green, and yon crystalline sky,
Announce a season potent to renew,
'Mid frost and snow, the instinctive joys of song,
And nobler cares than listless summer knew.

THERE is a pleasure in poetic pains
Which only Poets know;—'twas rightly said;
Whom could the Muses else allure to tread
Their smoothest paths, to wear their lightest chains?
When happiest Fancy has inspired the strains,
How oft the malice of one luckless word
Pursues the Enthusiast to the social board,
Haunts him belated on the silent plains!
Yet he repines not, if his thought stand clear,
At last, of hind'rance and obscurity.
Fresh as the star that crowns the brow of morn;
Bright, speckless, as a softly-moulded tear
The moment it has left the virgin's eye,
Or rain-drop lingering on the pointed thorn.

ALFRED PARSONS.

Y E sacred Nurseries of blooming Youth!
In whose collegiate shelter England's Flowers
Expand, enjoying through their vernal hours
The air of liberty, the light of truth;
Much have ye suffered from Time's gnawing tooth:
Yet, O ye Spires of Oxford! domes and towers!
Gardens and groves! your presence overpowers
The soberness of reason; till, in sooth,
Transformed, and rushing on a bold exchange,
I slight my own beloved Cam, to range
Where silver Isis leads my stripling feet;
Pace the long avenue, or glide adown
The stream-like windings of that glorious street—
An eager Novice robed in fluttering gown!

A *PARSONAGE IN OXFORDSHIRE.*

WHERE holy ground begins, unhallowed ends,
Is marked by no distinguishable line;
The turf unites, the pathways intertwine;
And, wheresoe'er the stealing footstep tends,
Garden, and that domain where kindred, friends,
And neighbours rest together, here confound
Their several features, mingled like the sound
Of many waters, or as evening blends
With shady night. Soft airs, from shrub and flower,
Waft fragrant greetings to each silent grave;
And while those lofty poplars gently wave
Their tops, between them comes and goes a sky
Bright as the glimpses of eternity,
To saints accorded in their mortal hour.

HAIL, Twilight, sovereign of one peaceful hour!
Not dull art thou as undiscerning Night;
But studious only to remove from sight
Day's mutable distinctions. Ancient Power!
Thus did the waters gleam, the mountains lower,
To the rude Briton, when, in wolf-skin vest
Here roving wild, he laid him down to rest
On the bare rock, or through a leafy bower
Looked ere his eyes were closed. By him was seen
The self-same Vision which we now behold,
At thy meek bidding, shadowy Power! brought forth
These mighty barriers, and the gulf between;
The flood, the stars—a spectacle as old
As the beginning of the heavens and earth!

MARK the concentred hazels that enclose
Yon old gray Stone, protected from the ray
Of noontide suns: and even the beams that play
And glance, while wantonly the rough wind blows,
Are seldom free to touch the moss that grows
Upon that roof, amid embowering gloom,
The very image framing of a Tomb,
In which some ancient Chieftain finds repose
Among the lonely mountains. Live, ye trees!
And thou, gray Stone, the pensive likeness keep
Of a dark chamber where the Mighty sleep:
For more than Fancy to the influence bends
When solitary Nature condescends
To mimic Time's forlorn humanities.

COMPOSED AT RYDAL ON MAY MORNING,
1838.

F with old love of you, dear Hills! I share
New love of many a rival image brought
From far, forgive the wanderings of my thought:
Nor art thou wronged, sweet May! when I compare
Thy present birth-morn with thy last, so fair,
So rich to me in favours. For my lot
Then was, within the famed Egerian Grot
To sit and muse, fanned by its dewy air
Mingling with thy soft breath! That morning, too,
Warblers I heard their joy unbosoming
Amid the sunny, shadowy Coliseum;
Heard them, unchecked by aught of saddening hue,
For victories there won by flower-crowned Spring,
Chant in full choir their innocent Te Deum.

THOUGH the bold wings of Poesy affect
    The clouds, and wheel around the mountain-tops
Rejoicing, from her loftiest height she drops
Well pleased to skim the plain with wild flowers deckt,
Or muse in solemn grove whose shades protect
The lingering dew—there steals along, or stops
Watching the least small bird that round her hops,
Or creeping worm, with sensitive respect.
Her functions are they therefore less divine,
Her thoughts less deep, or void of grave intent
Her simplest fancies? Should that fear be thine,
Aspiring Votary, ere thy hand present
One offering, kneel before her modest shrine
With brow in penitential sorrow bent!

22

PELION and Ossa flourish side by side,
   Together in immortal books enrolled:
   His ancient dower Olympus hath not sold;
   And that inspiring Hill, which "did divide
Into two ample horns his forehead wide,"
Shines with poetic radiance as of old;
While not an English Mountain we behold
By the celestial Muses glorified.
Yet round our sea-girt shore they rise in crowds:
What was the great Parnassus' self to Thee,
Mount Skiddaw? In his natural sovereignty
Our British Hill is nobler far; he shrouds
His double front among Atlantic clouds,
And pours forth streams more sweet than Castaly.

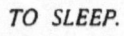

TO SLEEP.

FLOCK of sheep that leisurely pass by,
One after one; the sound of rain, and bees
Murmuring; the fall of rivers, winds and seas,
Smooth fields, white sheets of water, and pure sky;
I have thought of all by turns, and yet do lie
Sleepless! and soon the small birds' melodies
Must hear, first uttered from my orchard trees;
And the first cuckoo's melancholy cry.
Even thus last night, and two nights more, I lay,
And could not win thee, Sleep! by any stealth:
So do not let me wear to-night away:
Without Thee what is all the morning's wealth?
Come, blessed barrier between day and day,
Dear mother of fresh thoughts and joyous health!

FOND words have oft been spoken to thee, Sleep!
    And thou hast had thy store of tenderest names;
The very sweetest Fancy culls or frames
When thankfulness of heart is strong and deep!
Dear Bosom-child we call thee, that dost steep
In rich reward all suffering; Balm that tames
All anguish; Saint that evil thoughts and aims
Takest away, and into souls dost creep,
Like to a breeze from heaven. Shall I alone,
I surely not a man ungently made,
Call thee worst Tyrant by which Flesh is crost?
Perverse, self-willed to own and to disown,
Mere slave of them who never for thee prayed,
Still last to come where thou art wanted most!

EDEN! till now thy beauty had I viewed
By glimpses only, and confess with shame
That verse of mine, whate'er its varying mood,
Repeats but once the sound of thy sweet name:
Yet fetched from Paradise that honour came,
Rightfully borne; for Nature gives thee flowers
That have no rivals among British bowers;
And thy bold rocks are worthy of their fame.
Measuring thy course, fair Stream! at length I pay
To my life's neighbour dues of neighbourhood;
But I have traced thee on thy winding way
With pleasure sometimes by this thought restrained—
For things far off we toil, while many a good
Not sought, because too near, is never gained.

SURPRISED by joy—impatient as the Wind
I turned to share the transport—Oh! with whom
But Thee, deep buried in the silent tomb,
That spot which no vicissitude can find?
Love, faithful love, recalled thee to my mind—
But how could I forget thee? Through what power,
Even for the least division of an hour,
Have I been so beguiled as to be blind ·
To my most grievous loss?—That thought's return
Was the worst pang that sorrow ever bore,
Save one, one only, when I stood forlorn,
Knowing my heart's best treasure was no more;
That neither present time nor years unborn
Could to my sight that heavenly face restore.

ER only pilot the soft breeze, the boat
Lingers, but Fancy is well satisfied;
With keen-eyed Hope, with Memory, at her side,
And the glad Muse at liberty to note
All that to each is precious, as we float
Gently along; regardless who shall chide
If the heavens smile, and leave us free to glide,
Happy Associates breathing air remote
From trivial cares.   But, Fancy and the Muse,
Why have I crowded this small bark with you
And others of your kind, ideal crew!
While here sits One whose brightness owes its hues
To flesh and blood; no Goddess from above,
No fleeting Spirit, but my own true.Love?

WITH Ships the sea was sprinkled far and nigh,
Like stars in heaven, and joyously it showed;
Some lying fast at anchor in the road,
Some veering up and down, one knew not why.
A goodly Vessel did I then espy
Come like a giant from a haven broad;
And lustily along the bay she strode,
Her tackling rich, and of apparel high.
This Ship was naught to me, nor I to her,
Yet I pursued her with a Lover's look;
This ship to all the rest did I prefer:
When will she turn, and whither? She will brook
No tarrying; where She comes the winds must stir:
On went She, and due north her journey took.

WHERE lies the Land to which yon Ship must go?
Fresh as a lark mounting at break of day,
Festively she puts forth in trim array;
Is she for tropic suns, or polar snow?
What boots the inquiry?—Neither friend nor foe
She cares for; let her travel where she may,
She finds familiar names, a beaten way
Ever before her, and a wind to blow.
Yet still I ask, what haven is her mark?
And, almost as it was when ships were rare,
(From time to time, like Pilgrims, here and there
Crossing the waters) doubt, and something dark,
Of the old Sea some reverential fear,
Is with me at thy farewell, joyous Bark!

THE RIVER DUDDON.

SOLE listener, Duddon! to the Breeze that played
With thy clear voice, I caught the fitful sound
Wafted o'er sullen moss and craggy mound—
Unfruitful solitudes, that seemed to upbraid
The sun in heaven!—but now, to form a shade
For Thee, green alders have together wound
Their foliage; ashes flung their arms around;
And birch-trees risen in silver colonnade.
And thou hast also tempted here to rise,
'Mid sheltering pines, this Cottage rude and gray;
Whose ruddy children, by the mother's eyes
Carelessly watched, sport through the summer day,
Thy pleased Associates:—light as endless May
On infant bosoms lonely Nature lies.

WHAT aspect bore the Man who roved or fled,
    First of his tribe, to this dark dell—who first
In this pellucid Current slaked his thirst?
What hopes came with him? what designs were spread
Along his path? His unprotected bed
What dreams encompassed? Was the intruder nursed
In hideous usages, and rites accursed,
That thinned the living and disturbed the dead?
No voice replies;—both air and earth are mute;
And Thou, blue Streamlet, murmuring yield'st no more
Than a soft record, that, whatever fruit
Of ignorance thou mightst witness heretofore,
Thy function was to heal and to restore,
To soothe and cleanse, not madden and pollute!

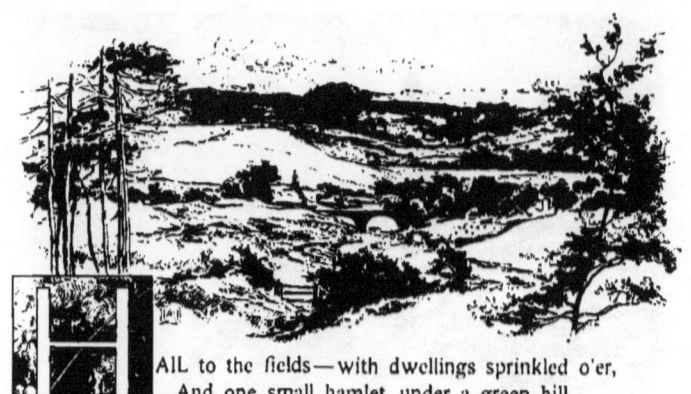

HAIL to the fields—with dwellings sprinkled o'er,
    And one small hamlet, under a green hill
    Clustering, with barn and byre, and spouting mill!
A glance suffices;—should we wish for more,
Gay June would scorn us. But when bleak winds roar
Through the stiff, lance-like shoots of pollard ash,
Dread swell of sound! loud as the gusts that lash
The matted forests of Ontario's shore
By wasteful steel unsmitten—then would I
Turn into port; and, reckless of the gale,
Reckless of angry Duddon sweeping by,
While the warm hearth exalts the mantling ale,
Laugh with the generous household heartily
At all the merry pranks of Donnerdale!

The River Duddon
The Stepping Stones

THE struggling Rill insensibly is grown
   Into a Brook of loud and stately march,
   Crossed ever and anon by plank or arch;
And, for like use, lo! what might seem a zone
Chosen for ornament—stone matched with stone
In studied symmetry, with interspace
For the clear waters to pursue their race
Without restraint. How swiftly have they flown,
Succeeding—still succeeding! Here the Child
Puts, when the high-swoln Flood runs fierce and wild,
His budding courage to the proof; and here
Declining Manhood learns to note the sly
And sure encroachments of infirmity,
Thinking how fast time runs, life's end how near!

33

WHENCE that low voice?—A whisper from the heart,
That told of days long past, when here I roved
With friends and kindred tenderly beloved;
Some who had early mandates to depart,
Yet are allowed to steal my path athwart
By Duddon's side; once more do we unite,
Once more, beneath the kind Earth's tranquil light;
And smothered joys into new being start.
From her unworthy seat, the cloudy stall
Of Time, breaks forth triumphant Memory;
Her glistening tresses bound, yet light and free
As golden locks of birch, that rise and fall
On gales that breathe too gently to recall
Aught of the fading year's inclemency!

I THOUGHT of Thee, my partner and my guide,
As being passed away.—Vain sympathies!
For, backward, Duddon, as I cast my eyes,
I see what was, and is, and will abide;
Still glides the Stream, and shall forever glide;
The Form remains, the Function never dies;
While we, the brave, the mighty, and the wise,
We Men, who in our morn of youth defied
The elements, must vanish;—be it so!
Enough, if something from our hands have power
To live, and act, and serve the future hour;
And if, as toward the silent tomb we go,
Through love, through hope, and faith's transcendent dower,
We feel that we are greater than we know.

BROOK! whose society the poet seeks,
Intent his wasted spirits to renew;
And whom the curious Painter doth pursue
Through rocky passes, among flowery creeks,
And tracks thee dancing down thy waterbreaks;
If wish were mine some type of thee to view,
Thee, and not thee thyself, I would not do
Like Grecian Artists, give thee human cheeks,
Channels for tears; no Naiad shouldst thou be—
Have neither limbs, feet, feathers, joints, nor hairs:
It seems the Eternal Soul is clothed in thee
With purer robes than those of flesh and blood,
And hath bestowed on thee a safer good;
Unwearied joy, and life without its cares.

METHINKS that to some vacant hermitage
   My feet would rather turn—to some dry nook
Scooped out of living rock, and near a brook
Hurled down a mountain-cove from stage to stage,
Yet tempering, for my sight, its bustling rage
In the soft heaven of a translucent pool;
Thence creeping under sylvan arches cool,
Fit haunt of shapes whose glorious equipage
Would elevate my dreams. A beechen bowl,
A maple dish, my furniture should be;
Crisp, yellow leaves my bed; the hooting owl
My night-watch: nor should e'er the crested fowl
From thorp or vill his matins sound for me,
Tired of the world and all its industry.

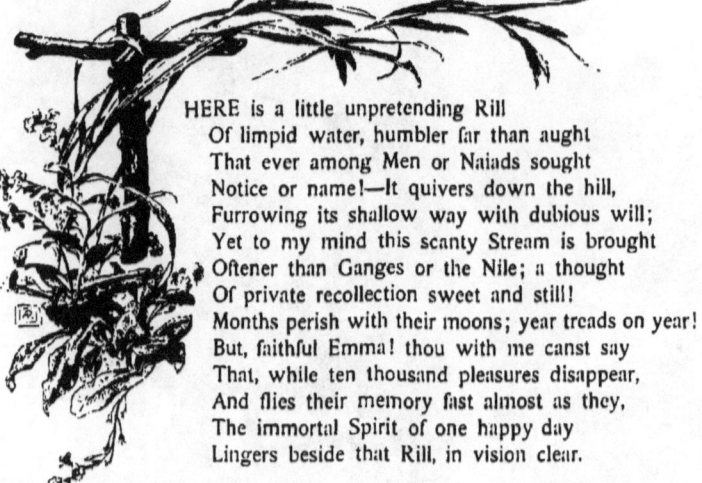

HERE is a little unpretending Rill
   Of limpid water, humbler far than aught
   That ever among Men or Naiads sought
Notice or name!—It quivers down the hill,
Furrowing its shallow way with dubious will;
Yet to my mind this scanty Stream is brought
Oftener than Ganges or the Nile; a thought
Of private recollection sweet and still!
Months perish with their moons; year treads on year!
But, faithful Emma! thou with me canst say
That, while ten thousand pleasures disappear,
And flies their memory fast almost as they,
The immortal Spirit of one happy day
Lingers beside that Rill, in vision clear.

WRITTEN UPON A BLANK LEAF
IN "THE COMPLETE ANGLER."

WHILE flowing rivers yield a blameless sport,
Shall live the name of Walton: Sage benign!
Whose pen, the mysteries of the rod and line
Unfolding, did not fruitlessly exhort
To reverend watching of each still report
That Nature utters from her rural shrine.
Meek, nobly versed in simple discipline,
He found the longest summer day too short,
To his loved pastime given by sedgy Lee,
Or down the tempting maze of Shawford brook—
Fairer than life itself, in this sweet Book,
The cowslip bank and shady willow-tree;
And the fresh meads—where flowed, from every nook
Of his full bosom, gladsome Piety!

O FRIEND! I know not which way I must look
For comfort, being, as I am, opprest,
To think that now our life is only drest
For show; mean handiwork of craftsman, cook,
Or groom!—We must run glittering like a brook
In the open sunshine, or we are unblest:
The wealthiest man among us is the best:
No grandeur now in nature or in book
Delights us. Rapine, avarice, expense,
This is idolatry; and these we adore:
Plain living and high thinking are no more:
The homely beauty of the good old cause
Is gone; our peace, our fearful innocence,
And pure religion breathing household laws.

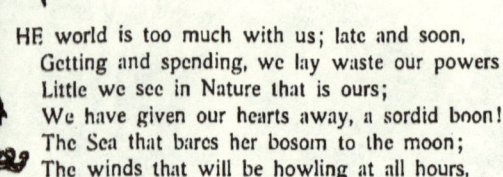

THE world is too much with us; late and soon,
Getting and spending, we lay waste our powers:
Little we see in Nature that is ours;
We have given our hearts away, a sordid boon!
The Sea that bares her bosom to the moon;
The winds that will be howling at all hours,
And are up-gathered now like sleeping flowers;
For this, for everything, we are out of tune;
It moves us not. —Great God! I'd rather be
A Pagan suckled in a creed outworn;
So might I, standing on this pleasant lea,
Have glimpses that would make me less forlorn;
Have sight of Proteus rising from the sea;
Or hear old Triton blow his wreathèd horn.

ILTON! thou shouldst be living at this hour:
England hath need of thee: she is a fen
Of stagnant waters: altar, sword, and pen,
Fireside, the heroic wealth of hall and bower,
Have forfeited their ancient English dower
Of inward happiness. We are selfish men;
Oh! raise us up, return to us again;
And give us manners, virtue, freedom, power,
Thy soul was like a Star, and dwelt apart:
Thou hadst a voice whose sound was like the sea:
Pure as the naked heavens, majestic, free,
So didst thou travel on life's common way,
In cheerful godliness; and yet thy heart
The lowliest duties on herself did lay.

GREAT men have been among us; hands that penned
And tongues that uttered wisdom—better none:
The later Sidney, Marvel, Harrington,
Young Vane, and others who called Milton friend.
These moralists could act and comprehend:
They knew how genuine glory was put on;
Taught us how rightfully a nation shone
In splendour: what strength was, that would not bend
But in magnanimous meekness. France, tis strange,
Hath brought forth no such souls as we had then.
Perpetual emptiness! unceasing change!
No single volume paramount, no code,
No master spirit, no determined road;
But equally a want of books and men!

IT is not to be thought of that the Flood
Of British Freedom, which, to the open sea
Of the world's praise, from dark antiquity
Hath flowed, "with pomp of waters, unwithstood,"
Roused though it be full often to a mood
Which spurns the check of salutary bands,
That this most famous Stream in bogs and sands
Should perish; and to evil and to good
Be lost forever. In our halls is hung
Armoury of the invincible Knights of old:
We must be free or die, who speak the tongue
That Shakspeare spake; the faith and morals hold
Which Milton held. —In everything we are sprung
Of Earth's first blood, have titles manifold.

WHEN I have borne in memory what has tamed
Great Nations, how ennobling thoughts depart
When men change swords for ledgers, and desert
The Student's bower for gold, some fears unnamed
I had, my Country!—am I to be blamed?
Now, when I think of thee, and what thou art,
Verily, in the bottom of my heart,
Of those unfilial fears I am ashamed.
For dearly must we prize thee; we who find
In thee a bulwark for the cause of men:
And I by my affection was beguiled:
What wonder if a Poet now and then,
Among the many movements of his mind,
Felt for thee as a lover or a child!

45

INLAND, within a hollow vale, I stood;
And saw, while sea was calm and air was clear,
The coast of France—the coast of France how near!
Drawn almost into frightful neighbourhood.
I shrunk; for verily the barrier flood
Was like a lake, or river bright and fair,
A span of waters; yet what power is there!
What mightiness for evil and for good!
Even so does God protect us if we be
Virtuous and wise. Winds blow, and waters roll,
Strength to the brave, and Power, and Deity;
Yet in themselves are nothing! One decree
Spake laws to *them*, and said that by the soul
Only, the Nations shall be great and free.

VANGUARD of Liberty, ye men of Kent,
Ye children of a Soil that doth advance
Her haughty brow against the coast of France,
Now is the time to prove your hardiment!
To France be words of invitation sent!
They from their fields can see the countenance
Of your fierce war, may ken the glittering lance
And hear you shouting forth your brave intent.
Left single, in bold parley, ye, of yore,
Did from the Norman win a gallant wreath;
Confirmed the charters that were yours before;—
No parleying now! In Britain is one breath;
We all are with you now from shore to shore;—
Ye men of Kent, 'tis victory or death!

THOUGHT OF A BRITON ON THE SUBJUGATION OF SWITZERLAND.

TWO voices are there; one is of the sea,
One of the mountains; each a mighty Voice:
In both from age to age thou didst rejoice,
They were thy chosen music, Liberty!
There came a Tyrant, and with holy glee
Thou fought'st against him; but hast vainly striven:
Thou from thy Alpine holds at length art driven,
Where not a torrent murmurs heard by thee.
Of one deep bliss thine ear hath been bereft:
Then cleave, O cleave to that which still is left;
For, high-souled Maid, what sorrow would it be
That Mountain floods should thunder as before,
And Ocean bellow from his rocky shore,
And neither awful voice be heard by thee!

AN INVASION BEING EXPECTED, OCTOBER.
1803.

SIX thousand veterans practised in war's game,
Tried men, at Killicranky were arrayed
Against an equal host that wore the plaid,
Shepherds and herdsmen.—Like a whirlwind came
The Highlanders, the slaughter spread like flame;
And Garry, thundering down his mountain-road,
Was stopped, and could not breathe beneath the load
Of the dead bodies.—'Twas a day of shame
For them whom precept and the pedantry
Of cold mechanic battle do enslave.
O for a single hour of that Dundee,
Who on that day the word of onset gave!
Like conquest would the Men of England see;
And her Foes find a like inglorious grave.

47.

COMPOSED IN THE VALLEY NEAR DOVER, ON THE DAY OF LANDING.

HERE, on our native soil, we breathe once more.
The cock that crows, the smoke that curls, that sound
Of bells; those boys who in yon meadow-ground
In white-sleeved shirts are playing; and the roar
Of the waves breaking on the chalky shore;—
All, all are English. Oft have I looked round
With joy in Kent's green vales; but never found
Myself so satisfied in heart before.
Europe is yet in bonds; but let that pass,
Thought for another moment. Thou art free,
My Country! and 'tis joy enough and pride
For one hour's perfect bliss, to tread the grass
Of England once again, and hear and see,
With such a dear Companion at my side.

NOT Love, not War, nor the tumultuous swell,
Of civil conflict, nor the wrecks of change,
Nor Duty struggling with afflictions strange—
Not these *alone* inspired the tuneful shell;
But where untroubled peace and concord dwell,
There also is the Muse not loath to range,
Watching the twilight smoke of cot or grange,
Skyward ascending from a woody dell.
Meek aspirations please her, lone endeavour,
And sage content, and placid melancholy;
She loves to gaze upon a crystal river—
Diaphanous because it travels slowly;
Soft is the music that would charm forever;
The flower of sweetest smell is shy and lowly.

TO

TOUSSAINT L'OUVERTURE.

OUSSAINT, the most unhappy man of men!
　　Whether the whistling Rustic tend his plough
　　Within thy hearing, or thy head be now
　　Pillowed in some deep dungeon's earless den;—
　　O miserable Chieftain! where and when
　　Wilt thou find patience? Yet die not; do thou
　　Wear rather in thy bonds a cheerful brow:
　　Though fallen thyself, never to rise again,
　　Live, and take comfort. Thou hast left behind
Powers that will work for thee; air, earth, and skies;
There's not a breathing of the common wind
That will forget thee; thou hast great allies;
Thy friends are exultations, agonies,
And love, and man's unconquerable mind.

WHEN Philoctetes in the Lemnian isle
　　Like a form sculptured on a monument
Lay couched; on him or his dread bow unbent
Some wild bird oft might settle and beguile
The rigid features of a transient smile,
Disperse the tear, or to the sigh give vent,
Slackening the pains of ruthless banishment
From his loved home, and from heroic toil.
And trust that spiritual Creatures round us move,
Griefs to allay which Reason cannot heal;
Yea, veriest reptiles have sufficed to prove
To fettered wretchedness, that no Bastile
Is deep enough to exclude the light of love,
Though man for brother man has ceased to feel.

WHEN haughty expectations prostrate lie,
        And grandeur crouches like a guilty thing,
        Oft shall the lowly weak, till Nature bring
        Mature release, in fair society
        Survive, and Fortune's utmost anger try;
        Like these frail snow-drops that together cling,
And nod their helmets, smitten by the wing
Of many a furious whirl-blast sweeping by.
Observe the faithful flowers! if small to great
May lead the thoughts, thus struggling used to stand
The Emathian phalanx, nobly obstinate;
And so the bright immortal Theban band,
Whom onset, fiercely urged at Jove's command,
Might overwhelm, but could not separate!

O'ER the wide earth, on mountain and on plain,
        Dwells in the affections and the soul of man
A Godhead, like the universal PAN;
But more exalted, with a brighter train:
And shall his bounty be dispensed in vain,
Showered equally on city and on field,
And neither hope nor steadfast promise yield
In these usurping times of fear and pain?
Such doom awaits us. Nay, forbid it Heaven!
We know the arduous strife, the eternal laws
To which the triumph of all good is given,
High sacrifice, and labour without pause,
Even to the death:—else wherefore should the eye
Of man converse with immortality?

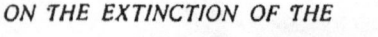

ONCE did she hold the gorgeous East in fee,
And was the safeguard of the West: the worth
Of Venice did not fall below her birth,
Venice, the eldest Child of Liberty.
She was a maiden City, bright and free;
No guile seduced, no force could violate;
And, when she took unto herself a Mate,
She must espouse the everlasting Sea.
And what if she had seen those glories fade,
Those titles vanish, and that strength decay;
Yet shall some tribute of regret be paid
When her long life hath reached its final day:
Men are we, and must grieve when even the Shade
Of that which once was great is passed away.

BY GRASMERE LAKE.

CLOUDS, lingering yet, extend in solid bars
Through the gray west; and lo! these waters, steeled
By breezeless air to smoothest polish, yield
A vivid repetition of the stars;
Jove, Venus, and the ruddy crest of Mars
Amid his fellows beauteously revealed
At happy distance from Earth's groaning field,
Where ruthless mortals wage incessant wars.
Is it a mirror?—or the nether Sphere
Opening to view the abyss in which she feeds
Her own calm fires?—But list! a voice is near;
Great Pan himself low-whispering through the reeds,
"Be thankful, thou; for, if unholy deeds
Ravage the world, tranquillity is here!"

COMPOSED BY THE SEA-SIDE, NEAR CALAIS.

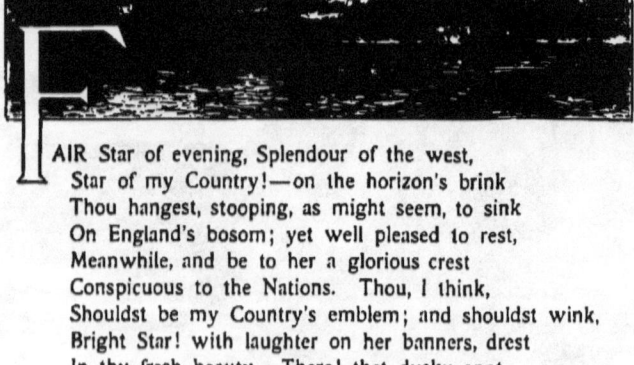

FAIR Star of evening, Splendour of the west,
Star of my Country!—on the horizon's brink
Thou hangest, stooping, as might seem, to sink
On England's bosom; yet well pleased to rest,
Meanwhile, and be to her a glorious crest
Conspicuous to the Nations. Thou, I think,
Shouldst be my Country's emblem; and shouldst wink,
Bright Star! with laughter on her banners, drest
In thy fresh beauty. There! that dusky spot
Beneath thee, that is England; there she lies.
Blessings be on you both! one hope, one lot,
One life, one glory!—I, with many a fear
For my dear Country, many heart-felt sighs,
.Among men who do not love her, linger here.

AS LEAVES are to the tree whereon they grow
And wither, every human generation
Is, to the Being of a mighty nation,
Locked in our world's embrace through weal and woe;
Thought that should teach the zealot to forego
Rash schemes, to abjure all selfish agitation,
And seek through noiseless pains and moderation
The unblemished good they only can bestow.
.Alas! with most, who weigh futurity
Against time present, passion holds the scales:
Hence equal ignorance of both prevails,
And nations sink; or, struggling to be free,
Are doomed to flounder on, like wounded whales
Tossed on the bosom of a stormy sea.

54

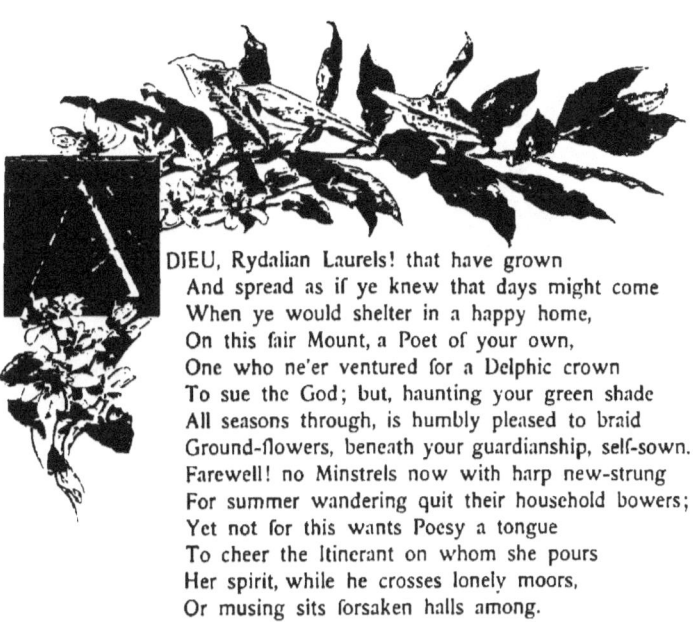

ADIEU, Rydalian Laurels! that have grown
And spread as if ye knew that days might come
When ye would shelter in a happy home,
On this fair Mount, a Poet of your own,
One who ne'er ventured for a Delphic crown
To sue the God; but, haunting your green shade
All seasons through, is humbly pleased to braid
Ground-flowers, beneath your guardianship, self-sown.
Farewell! no Minstrels now with harp new-strung
For summer wandering quit their household bowers;
Yet not for this wants Poesy a tongue
To cheer the Itinerant on whom she pours
Her spirit, while he crosses lonely moors,
Or musing sits forsaken halls among.

THE TROSACHS.

HERE'S not a nook within this solemn Pass,
But were an apt confessional for One
Taught by his summer spent, his autumn gone,
That Life is but a tale of morning grass
Withered at eve. From scenes of art which chase
That thought away, turn, and with watchful eyes
Feed it 'mid Nature's old felicities,
Rocks, rivers, and smooth lakes more clear than glass
Untouched, unbreathed upon. Thrice happy quest,
If from a golden perch of aspen spray
(October's workmanship to rival May)
The pensive warbler of the ruddy breast
That moral sweeten by a heaven-taught lay,
Lulling the year, with all its cares, to rest!

ADMONITION.

WELL may'st thou halt, and gaze with brightening eye!
The lovely Cottage in the guardian nook
Hath stirred thee deeply; with its own dear brook,
Its own small pasture, almost its own sky!
But covet not the Abode;—forbear to sigh,
As many do, repining while they look;
Intruders who would tear from Nature's book
This precious leaf with harsh impiety.
Think what the home must be if it were thine,
Even thine, though few thy wants!—Roof, window, door,
The very flowers are sacred to the Poor,
The roses to the porch which they intwine;
Yea, all, that now enchants thee, from the day
On which it should be touched, would melt away.

56

HE forest huge of ancient Caledon
Is but a name, no more is Inglewood,
That swept from hill to hill, from flood to flood:
On her last thorn the nightly moon has shone;
Yet still, though unappropriate Wild be none,
Fair parks spread wide where Adam Bell might deign
With Clym o' the Clough, were they alive again,
To kill for merry feast their venison.
Nor wants the holy Abbot's gliding Shade
His church with monumental wreck bestrown;
The feudal Warrior-chief a Ghost unlaid,
Hath still his castle, though a skeleton,
That he may watch by night, and lessons con
Of power that perishes, and rights that fade.

AIX-LA-CHAPELLE.

WAS it to disenchant, and to undo,
That we approached the seat of Charlemaine?
To sweep from many an old romantic strain
That faith which no devotion may renew!
Why does this puny Church present to view
Her feeble columns? and that scanty chair!
This sword that one of our weak times might wear!
Objects of false pretence, or meanly true!
If from a traveller's fortune I might claim
A palpable memorial of that day,
Then would I seek the Pyrenean Breach
That ROLAND clove with huge two-handed sway,
And to the enormous labour left his name,
Where unremitting frosts the rocky crescent bleach.

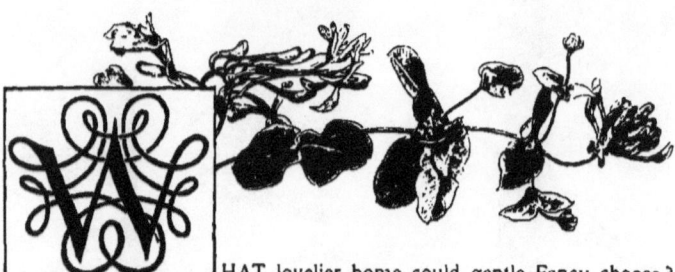

HAT lovelier home could gentle Fancy choose?
Is this the stream whose cities, heights, and plains,
War's favourite playground, are with crimson stains
Familiar, as the Morn with pearly dews?
The Morn, that now, along the silver MEUSE,
Spreading her peaceful ensigns, calls the swains
To tend their silent boats and ringing wains,
Or strip the bough whose mellow fruit bestrews
The ripening corn beneath it. As mine eyes
Turn from the fortified and threatening hill,
How sweet the prospect of yon watery glade,
With its gray rocks clustering in pensive shade—
That, shaped like old monastic turrets, rise
From the smooth meadow-ground, serene and still!

COMPOSED ON WESTMINSTER BRIDGE, SEPT. 3, 1802.

ARTH has not anything to show more fair:
Dull would he be of soul who could pass by
A sight so touching in its majesty:
This City now doth, like a garment, wear
The beauty of the morning; silent, bare,
Ships, towers, domes, theatres, and temples lie
Open unto the fields, and to the sky;
All bright and glittering in the smokeless air.
Never did sun more beautifully steep,
In his first splendour, valley, rock, or hill;
Ne'er saw I, never felt, a calm so deep!
The river glideth at his own sweet will:
Dear God! the very houses seem asleep;
And all that mighty heart is lying still!

ROMAN ANTIQUITIES.

HOW profitless the relics that we cull,
Troubling the last holds of ambitious Rome,
Unless they chasten fancies that presume
Too high, or idle agitations lull!
Of the world's flatteries if the brain be full,
To have no seat for thought were better doom,
Like this old helmet, or the eyeless skull
Of him who gloried in its nodding plume.
Heaven out of view, our wishes what are they?
Our fond regrets tenacious in their grasp?
The Sage's theory? the Poet's lay?
Mere Fibulæ without a robe to clasp;
Obsolete lamps, whose light no time recalls;
Urns without ashes, tearless lachrymals!

The Monument commonly called Long Meg and Her Daughters, near the River Eden.

A WEIGHT of awe, not easy to be borne,
Fell suddenly upon my Spirit—cast
From the dread bosom of the unknown past,
When first I saw that family forlorn.
Speak Thou, whose massy strength and stature scorn
The power of years—pre-eminent, and placed
Apart, to overlook the circle vast—
Speak, Giant-mother! tell it to the Morn
While she dispels the cumbrous shades of Night;
Let the Moon hear, emerging from a cloud;
At whose behest uprose on British ground
That Sisterhood, in hieroglyphic round
Forth-shadowing, some have deemed, the infinite,
The inviolable God, that tames the proud!

"HERE!" said a Stripling, pointing with meet pride
Towards a low roof with green trees half concealed,
"Is Mosgiel Farm; and that's the very field
Where Burns ploughed up the Daisy." Far and wide
A plain below stretched seaward, while, descried
Above sea-clouds, the Peaks of Arran rose;
And, by that simple notice, the repose
Of earth, sky, sea, and air was vivified.
Beneath "the random *bield* of clod or stone"
Myriads of daisies have shone forth in flower
Near the lark's nest, and in their natural hour
Have passed away; less happy than the One
That, by the unwilling ploughshare, died to prove
The tender charm of poetry and love.

MARY QUEEN OF SCOTS.

DEAR to the Loves, and to the Graces vowed,
The Queen drew back the wimple that she wore;
And to the throng, that on the Cumbrian shore
Her landing hailed, how touchingly she bowed!
And like a Star (that, from a heavy cloud
Of pine-tree foliage poised in air, forth darts,
When a soft summer gale at evening parts
The gloom that did its loveliness enshroud)
She smiled; but Time, the old Saturnian seer,
Sighed on the wing as her foot pressed the strand,
With step prelusive to a long array
Of woes and degradations hand in hand—
Weeping captivity, and shuddering fear
Stilled by the ensanguined block of Fotheringay!

In sight of the Town of Cockermouth.
(Where the Author was born, and his Father's remains are laid)

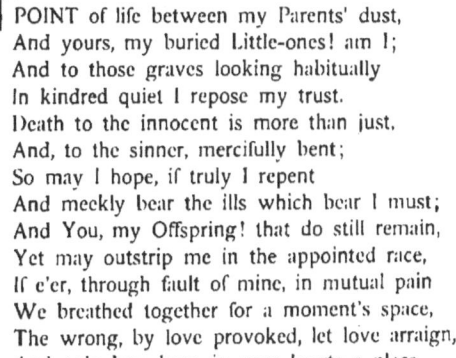

A POINT of life between my Parents' dust,
And yours, my buried Little-ones! am I;
And to those graves looking habitually
In kindred quiet I repose my trust.
Death to the innocent is more than just.
And, to the sinner, mercifully bent;
So may I hope, if truly I repent
And meekly bear the ills which bear I must;
And You, my Offspring! that do still remain,
Yet may outstrip me in the appointed race,
If e'er, through fault of mine, in mutual pain
We breathed together for a moment's space,
The wrong, by love provoked, let love arraign,
And only love keep in your hearts a place.

A PLACE OF BURIAL IN THE SOUTH OF
SCOTLAND.

PART fenced by man, part by a rugged steep
   That curbs a foaming brook, a Grave-yard lies;
The hare's best couching-place for fearless sleep;
Which moonlit elves, far seen by credulous eyes,
Enter in dance. Of church, or Sabbath ties,
No vestige now remains; yet thither creep
Bereft Ones, and in lowly anguish weep
Their prayers out to the wind and naked skies.
Proud tomb is none; but rudely-sculptured knights,
By humble choice of plain old times, are seen
Level with earth among the hillocks green:
Union not sad, when sunny daybreak smites
The spangled turf, and neighbouring thickets ring
With *jubilate* from the choirs of Spring!

MOST sweet it is with unuplifted eyes
   To pace the ground, if path be there or none,
While a fair region round the traveller lies
Which he forbears again to look upon;
Pleased rather with some soft ideal scene,
The work of Fancy, or some happy tone
Of meditation, slipping in between
The beauty coming and the beauty gone.
If Thought and Love desert us, from that day
Let us break off all commerce with the Muse:
With Thought and Love companions of our way,
Whate'er the senses take or may refuse,
The Mind's internal heaven shall shed her dews
Of inspiration on the humblest lay.

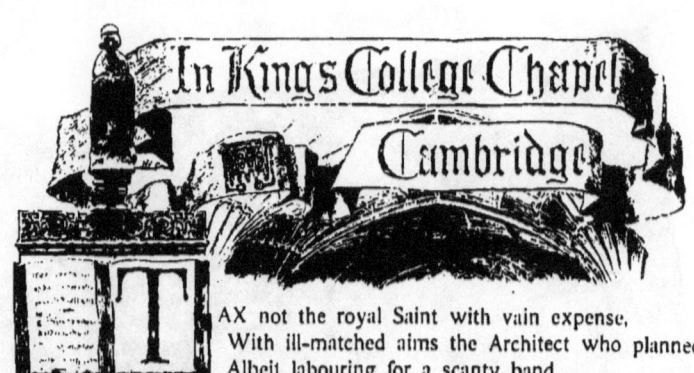

In Kings College Chapel Cambridge

TAX not the royal Saint with vain expense,
With ill-matched aims the Architect who planned—
Albeit labouring for a scanty band
Of white-robed Scholars only—this immense
And glorious Work of fine intelligence!
Give all thou canst; high Heaven rejects the lore
Of nicely-calculated less or more;
So deemed the man who fashioned for the sense
These lofty pillars, spread that branching roof
Self-poised, and scooped into ten thousand cells,
Where light and shade repose, where music dwells
Lingering—and wandering on as loath to die;
Like thoughts whose very sweetness yieldeth proof
That they were born for immortality.

THEY dreamt not of a perishable home
Who thus could build. Be mine, in hours of fear
Or grovelling thought, to seek a refuge here;
Or through the aisles of Westminster to roam:
Where bubbles burst, and folly's dancing foam
Melts, if it cross the threshold; where the wreath
Of awe-struck wisdom droops: or let my path
Lead to that younger Pile, whose sky-like dome
Hath typified by reach of daring art
Infinity's embrace; whose guardian crest,
The silent Cross, among the stars shall spread
As now, when She hath also seen her breast
Filled with mementos, satiate with its part
Of grateful England's overflowing Dead.

Rural Ceremony.

CLOSING the sacred Book which long has fed
  Our meditations, give we to a day
  Of annual joy one tributary lay;
  This day, when, forth by rustic music led,
  The village Children, while the sky is red
With evening lights, advance in long array
Through the still church-yard, each with garland gay,
That, carried sceptre-like, o'ertops the head
Of the proud Bearer. To the wide church-door,
Charged with these offerings which their fathers bore
For decoration in the Papal time,
The innocent procession softly moves:—
The spirit of Laud is pleased in heaven's pure clime,
And Hooker's voice the spectacle approves!

69

A STAR that shines dependent upon star
 Is to the sky while we look up in love;
  As to the deep fair ships which though they move
 Seem fixed to eyes that watch them from afar;
As to the sandy desert fountains are,
With palm-groves shaded at wide intervals,
Whose fruit around the sun-burnt Native falls
Of roving tired or desultory war—
Such to this British Isle her Christian Fanes,
Each linked to each for kindred services;
Her Spires, her Steeple-towers with glittering vanes
Far-kenned, her Chapels lurking among trees,
Where a few villagers on bended knees
Find solace which a busy world disdains.

WHO but is pleased to watch the moon on high
Travelling where she from time to time enshrouds
Her head, and nothing loath her Majesty
Renounces, till among the scattered clouds
One with its kindling edge declares that soon
Will reappear before the uplifted eye
A Form as bright, as beautiful a moon,
To glide in open prospect through clear sky.
Pity that such a promise e'er should prove
False in the issue, that yon seeming space
Of sky should be in truth the steadfast face
Of a cloud flat and dense, through which must move
(By transit not unlike man's frequent doom)
The Wanderer lost in more determined gloom.

THE Shepherd, looking eastward, softly said,
"Bright is thy veil, O Moon, as thou art bright!"
Forthwith, that little cloud, in ether spread
And penetrated all with tender light,
She cast away, and showed her fulgent head
Uncovered; dazzling the Beholder's sight
As if to vindicate her beauty's right
Her beauty thoughtlessly disparagèd.
Meanwhile that veil, removed or thrown aside,
Went floating from her, darkening as it went;
And a huge mass, to bury or to hide,
Approached this glory of the firmament;
Who meekly yields, and is obscured—content
With one calm triumph of a modest pride.

WITH how sad steps, O Moon, thou climb'st the sky,
"How silently, and with how wan a face!"
Where art thou? Thou so often seen on high
Running among the clouds a Wood-nymph's race!
Unhappy Nuns, whose common breath's a sigh
Which they would stifle, move at such a pace!
The northern Wind, to call thee to the chase,
Must blow to-night his bugle horn. Had I
The power of Merlin, Goddess! this should be:
And all the stars, fast as the clouds were riven,
Should sally forth, to keep thee company,
Hurrying and sparkling through the clear blue heaven;
But, Cynthia! should to thee the palm be given,
Queen both for beauty and for majesty.

THE stars are mansions built by Nature's hand,
And, haply, there the spirits of the blest
Dwell, clothed in radiance, their immortal vest;
Huge Ocean shows, within his yellow strand,
A habitation marvellously planned,
For life to occupy in love and rest;
All that we see is dome, or vault, or nest,
Or fortress, reared at Nature's sage command.
Glad thought for every season! but the Spring
Gave it while cares were weighing on my heart,
'Mid song of birds, and insects murmuring;
And while the youthful year's prolific art —
Of bud, leaf, blade, and flower — was fashioning
Abodes where self-disturbance hath no part.

To a Snow-drop

LONE Flower, hemmed in with snows
    and white as they
But hardier far, once more I see thee bend
Thy forehead, as if fearful to offend,
Like an unbidden guest. Though day by day,
Storms, sallying from the mountain-tops,
    waylay
The rising sun, and on the plains descend;
Yet art thou welcome, welcome as a friend
Whose zeal outruns his promise! Blue-eyed May
Shall soon behold this border thickly set
With bright jonquils, their odours lavishing
On the soft West-wind and his frolic peers;
Nor will I then thy modest grace forget,
Chaste Snow-drop, venturous harbinger of
    Spring,
And pensive monitor of fleeting years!

ARK! 'tis the Thrush, undaunted, undeprest,
   By twilight premature of cloud and rain;
   Nor does that roaring wind deaden his strain
   Who carols thinking of his Love and nest,
   And seems, as more incited, still more blest.
   Thanks; thou hast snapped a fireside Prisoner's chain,
Exulting Warbler! eased a fretted brain,
And in a moment charmed my cares to rest.
Yes, I will forth, bold Bird! and front the blast,
That we may sing together, if thou wilt,
So loud, so clear, my Partner through life's day,
Mute in her nest love-chosen, if not love-built
Like thine, shall gladden, as in seasons past,
Thrilled by loose snatches of the social Lay.

I DROPPED my pen; and listened to the Wind
   That sang of trees uptorn and vessels tost—
A midnight harmony; and wholly lost
To the general sense of men by chains confined
Of business, care, or pleasure; or resigned
To timely sleep. Thought I, the impassioned strain,
Which, without aid or numbers, I sustain,
Like acceptation from the World will find.
Yet some with apprehensive ear shall drink
A dirge devoutly breathed o'er sorrows past;
And to the attendant promise will give heed—
The prophecy—like that of this wild blast,
Which, while it makes the heart with sadness shrink,
Tells also of bright calms that shall succeed.

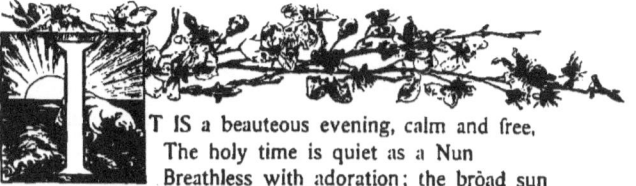

IT IS a beauteous evening, calm and free,
The holy time is quiet as a Nun
Breathless with adoration; the bròad sun
Is sinking down in its tranquillity;
The gentleness of heaven broods o'er the Sea:
Listen! the mighty Being is awake,
And doth with his eternal motion make
A sound like thunder—everlastingly.
Dear Child! dear Girl! that walkest with me here,
If thou appear untouched by solemn thought, .
Thy nature is not therefore less divine:
Thou liest in Abraham's bosom all the year;
And worshipp'st at the Temple's inner shrine,
God being with thee when we know it not.

TO THE CUCKOO.

NOT the whole warbling grove in concert heard,
    When sunshine follows shower, the breast can thrill
    Like the first summons, Cuckoo! of thy bill,
With its twin notes inseparably paired.
The captive 'mid damp vaults unsunned, unaired,
Measuring the periods of his lonely doom,
That cry can reach; and to the sick man's room
Sends gladness, by no languid smile declared.
The lordly eagle-race through hostile search
May perish; time may come when never more
The wilderness shall hear the lion roar;
But, long as cock shall crow from household perch
To rouse the dawn, soft gales shall speed thy wing,
And thy erratic voice be faithful to the Spring!

NEAR Anio's stream I spied a gentle Dove
    Perched on an olive-branch, and heard her cooing
'Mid new-born blossoms that soft airs were wooing,
While all things present told of joy and love.
But restless Fancy left that olive grove
To hail the exploratory Bird renewing
Hope for the few, who, at the world's undoing,
On the great flood were spared to live and move.
O bounteous Heaven! signs true as dove and bough
Brought to the ark are coming evermore, .
Given though we seek them not, but, while we plough
The sea of life without a visible shore, .
Do neither promise ask nor grace implore
In what alone is ours, the living Now.

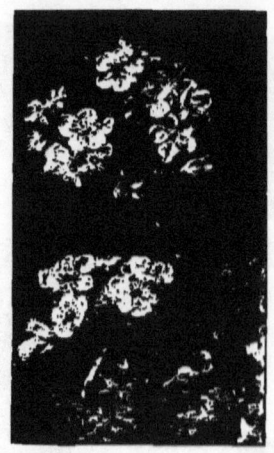

COMPOSED ON A MAY MORNING.

L IFE with yon Lambs, like day, is just begun,
   Yet Nature seems to them a heavenly guide,
Does joy approach? they meet the coming tide;
And sullenness avoid, as now they shun
Pale twilight's lingering glooms—and in the sun
Couch near their dams, with quiet satisfied;
Or gambol—each with his shadow at his side,
Varying its shape wherever he may run.
As they from turf yet hoar with sleepy dew
All turn, and court the shining and the green,
Where herbs look up, and opening flowers are seen;
Why to God's goodness can not We be true,
And so, His gifts and promises between,
Feed to the last on pleasures ever new?

I AM not one who much or oft delight
To season my fireside with personal talk—
Of friends, who live within an easy walk,
Or neighbours, daily, weekly, in my sight:
And, for my chance-acquaintance, ladies bright,
Sons, mothers, maidens withering on the stalk,
These all wear out of me, like Forms, with chalk
Painted on rich men's floors, for one feast-night.
Better than such discourse doth silence long,
Long, barren silence, square with my desire;
To sit without emotion, hope, or aim,
In the loved presence of my cottage-fire,
And listen to the flapping of the flame,
Or kettle whispering its faint undersong.

"YET life," you say, "is life; we have seen and see,
And with a living pleasure we describe;
And fits of sprightly malice do but bribe
The languid mind into activity.
Sound sense, and love itself, and mirth and glee
Are fostered by the comment and the gibe."
Even be it so; yet still among your tribe,
Our daily world's true Worldlings, rank not me!
Children are blest, and powerful; their world lies
More justly balanced; partly at their feet,
And part far from them: sweetest melodies
Are those that are by distance made more sweet;
Whose mind is but the mind of his own eyes,
He is a Slave; the meanest we can meet!

INGS have we—and as far as we can go,
We may find pleasure: wilderness and wood,
Blank ocean and mere sky, support that mood
Which with the lofty sanctifies the low.
Dreams, books, are each a world; and books, we know,
Are a substantial world, both pure and good:
Round these, with tendrils strong as flesh and blood,
Our pastime and our happiness will grow.
There find I personal themes, a plenteous store,
Matter wherein right voluble I am,
To which I listen with a ready ear;
Two shall be named, pre-eminently dear—
The gentle Lady married to the Moor;
And heavenly Una with her milk-white Lamb.

NOR can I not believe but that hereby
Great gains are mine; for thus I live remote
From evil speaking; rancour, never sought,
Comes to me not; malignant truth, or lie.
Hence have I genial seasons, hence have I
Smooth passions, smooth discourse, and joyous thought:
And thus from day to day my little boat
Rocks in its harbour, lodging peaceably.
Blessings be with them—and eternal praise,
Who gave us nobler loves, and nobler cares—
The Poets, who on earth have made us heirs
Of truth and pure delight by heavenly lays!
Oh! might my name be numbered among theirs,
Then gladly would I end my mortal days.

HOW sweet it is, when mother Fancy rocks
    The wayward brain, to saunter through a wood!
    An old place, full of many a lovely brood,
    Tall trees, green arbours, and ground-flowers in flocks;
And wild rose tiptoe upon hawthorn stocks,
Like a bold Girl, who plays her agile pranks
At Wakes and Fairs with wandering Mountebanks—
When she stands cresting the Clown's head, and mocks
The crowd beneath her. Verily I think
Such place to me is sometimes like a dream
Or map of the whole world: thoughts, link by link,
Enter through ears and eyesight, with such gleam
Of all things, that at last in fear I shrink,
And leap at once from the delicious stream.

HY art thou silent? Is thy love a plant
Of such weak fibre that the treacherous air
Of absence withers what was once so fair?
Is there no debt to pay, no boon to grant?
Yet have my thoughts for thee been vigilant—
Bound to thy service with unceasing care,
The mind's least generous wish a mendicant
For naught but what thy happiness could spare.
Speak—though this soft warm heart, once free to hold
A thousand tender pleasures, thine and mine,
Be left more desolate, more dreary cold
Than a forsaken bird's-nest filled with snow
'Mid its own bush of leafless eglantine—
Speak, that my torturing doubts their end may know!

HOUGH joy attend Thee orient at the birth
Of dawn, it cheers the lofty spirit most
To watch thy course when Daylight, fled from earth,
In the gray sky hath left his lingering Ghost,
Perplexed as if between a splendour lost
And splendour slowly mustering. Since the Sun,
The absolute, the world-absorbing One,
Relinquished half his empire to the host
Emboldened by thy guidance, holy Star,
Holy as princely—who that looks on thee,
Touching, as now, in thy humility
The mountain borders of this seat of care,
Can question that thy countenance is bright,
Celestial Power, as much with love as light?

VALEDICTORY SONNET.

ERVING no haughty Muse, my hands have here
    Disposed some cultured Flowerets (drawn from spots
Where they bloomed singly, or in scattered knots),
Each kind in several beds of one parterre ;
Both to allure the casual Loiterer,
And that, so placed, my Nurslings may requite
Studious regard with opportune delight,
Nor be unthanked, unless I fondly err.
But metaphor dismissed, and thanks apart,
Reader, farewell! My last words let them be—
If in this book Fancy and Truth agree;
If simple Nature trained by careful Art
Through It have won a passage to thy heart;
Grant me thy love, I crave no other fee!

WITH ILLUSTRATIONS BY ALFRED PARSONS.

"The Quiet Life." Certain Verses by Various Hands: the Motive set forth in a Prologue and Epilogue by AUSTIN DOBSON ; the whole Adorned with Numerous Drawings by EDWIN A. ABBEY and ALFRED PARSONS. 4to, Ornamental Leather, Gilt Edges, $7 50. (*In a Box.*)

Old Songs. With Drawings by EDWIN A. ABBEY and ALFRED PARSONS. With Mounted India Proof Frontispiece, left loose for framing. 4to, Ornamental Leather Cover, Gilt Edges, $7 50. (*In a Box.*)

She Stoops to Conquer; or, The Mistakes of a Night. A Comedy. By Dr. GOLDSMITH. With Ten Full-page Photo-gravure Reproductions, printed on separate Plates ; many Process Reproductions, and Wood-Engravings from Drawings by EDWIN A. ABBEY. Decorations by ALFRED PARSONS. Introduction by AUSTIN DOBSON. Folio, Illuminated Leather, Gilt Edges, $20 00. (*In a Box.*)

PUBLISHED BY HARPER & BROTHERS, NEW YORK.

☞ *Any of the above works will be sent by mail. postage prepaid, to any part of the United States, Canada, or Mexico, on receipt of the price.*

www.ingramcontent.com/pod-product-compliance
Lightning Source LLC
Chambersburg PA
CBHW020048030726
47499CB00007B/2634